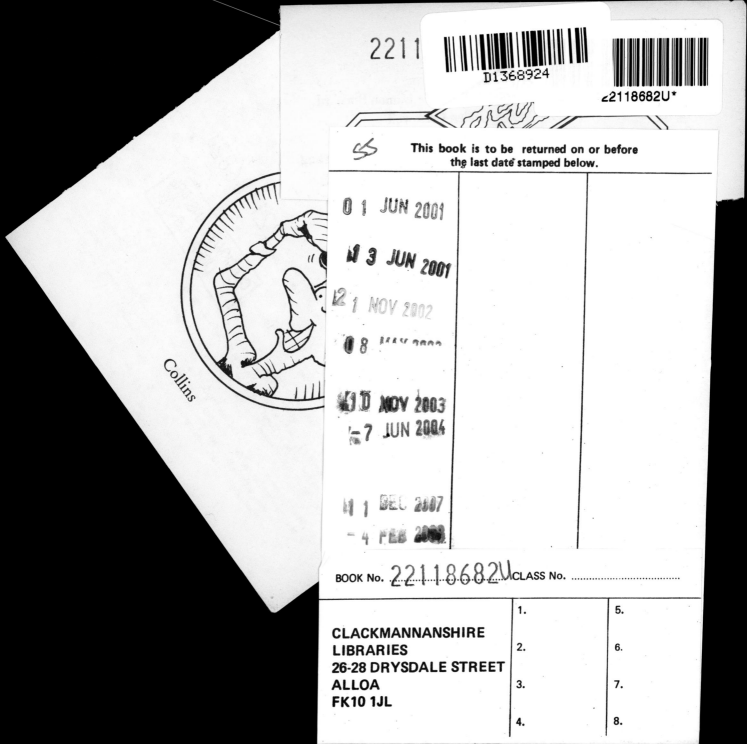

Collins

Look out for more Jets from Collins

Jessy Runs Away • Rachel Anderson
Ivana the Inventor • Best Friends •
Two Hoots • Almost Goodbye Guzzler • Ernest the Heroic Lion Tamer
Shadows on the Barn • **Sarah Garland**
Nora Bone • The Mystery of ...
Thing on Two Legs •
Desperate for a Dog ...

George and ... •
Cowardy Cowardy ...
Mo and the Mummy Case •
Mossop's Last Chance • Mum's the ...
Hiccup Harry • Harry Moves House • **Chr...**
Rattle and Hum, Robot Detectives • **Frank Rodger...**
Our Toilet's Haunted • **John Talbot**
Rhyming Russell • Messages • **Pat Thomson**
Monty the Dog Who Wears Glasses • Monty's Ups and Downs • **Colin West**
Ging Gang Goolie, it's an Alien • Stone the Crows, it's a Vacuum Cleaner •
Bob Wilson

First published by A & C Black Ltd in 1991
Published by Collins in 1992
10 9 8
Collins is an imprint of HarperCollins*Publishers*Ltd,
77–85 Fulham Palace Road, Hammersmith, London W6 8JB

ISBN 0 00 663824 4

Text and illustrations © Robin Kingsland 1991

Robin Kingsland asserts the moral right to
be identified as the author and the illustrator of the work.
A CIP record for this title is available from the British Library.
Printed and bound in Great Britain by
Caledonian International Book Manufacturing Ltd, Glasgow

Chapter One

St Anne's school had a brand new headteacher. His name was Mr Glottiss.

Nobody knew much about Mr Glottiss. Except that he *hated* music. And so when Mo Jones went to ask him a favour one day she was very, *very* nervous.

Every year at St Anne's there was
a school concert, and this year Mo
was playing a violin duet with her
next-door neighbour Glen Tring.

Mo stood in front of the dreaded
Head. She crossed her fingers
and said:

There was a strange noise,
like someone with hobnailed
boots treading on sugar:
Mr Glottiss was gritting
his teeth. It was what he
did when he was angry.

'The School Concert?' he gritted.
'The School Concert? All I hear
about is the School Concert! If I had
my way I'd . . .'

He stopped in mid-grit. Then he said,
'School is for lessons. The answer is

Mo stomped out of school and down Museum Street to wait for her bus.

You could have dropped a dinosaur on her for all she cared. She felt miserable.

Chapter Two

The museum manager wasn't very happy either. Two removal men were carrying a new mummy case up the stairs. So far they had managed to remove

three valuable vases,

four light bulbs,

and a museum guide's hat!

Somehow, they kept the mummy
case in one piece, *until* they went
through the door marked

The manager
scuttled over.

No-one noticed as a small, bright, glassy thing wobbled fell and

plinked

along

the

floor . . .

9

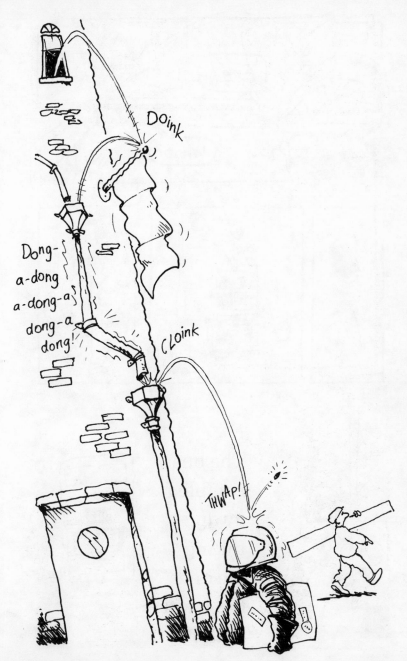

11

The bus
rumbled
away,
taking
Mo and
the jewel
with it.

Chapter Three

Late that night, the museum was
locked up and the night watchman
was in his cosy little office. (They
are called night watchmen
because they watch
telly all night.)

But up in the Egypt room, things
were happening. It was time for the
mummies' nightly inspection.

The oldest mummy of all, the
Great-Grandaddy mummy,
shuffled along the dusty line . . .

15

Suddenly the Great Grandaddy
mummy caught sight of Tut's
mummy case. 'Just a minute . . .'
he said. He peered closer.

All the mummies sucked in their
breath. Tut just looked blank.
A whisper ran through the parade.

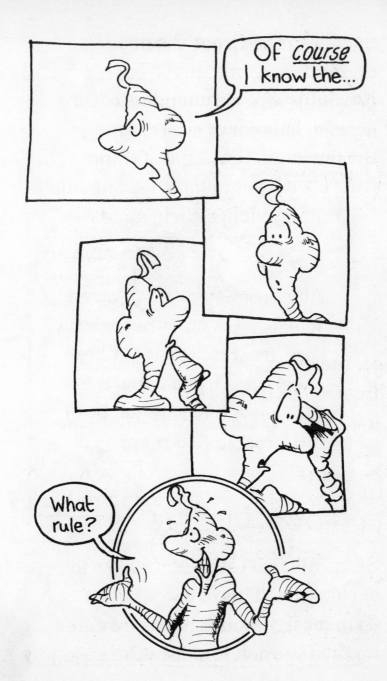

Chapter Four

Rules 1 to 4 of mummydom cover
general behaviour – no running in
the pyramid, that kind of thing.
Rule 6 we'll get to later . . . but rule
5 of mummydom clearly states:

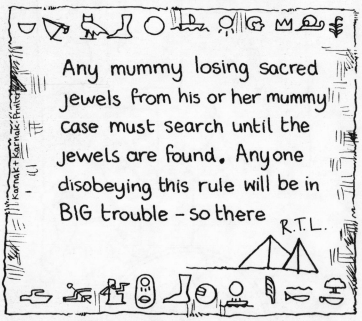

Any mummy losing sacred
jewels from his or her mummy
case must search until the
jewels are found. Anyone
disobeying this rule will be in
BIG trouble – so there

R.T.L.

Silly rule, isn't it? But then – a lot
of rules are. This one was sillier
than most, because it was invented
by the Pharaoh Rameses the Loopy.

Rameses was only Pharaoh for three days before people realised that he was off his rocker. But in that short time he wrote at least fifty-two idiotic rules. Rules like:

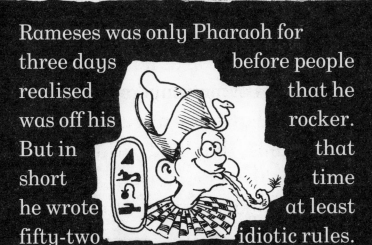

All pyramids should be covered in marshmallow because pink is a nice colour and no one will get hurt if they bump into one in the dark.

Mummies should be wrapped in crisp packets so that you can hear them if they creep up behind you.

Most of Rameses's rules were crossed out as soon as he'd been locked up. But for some reason rule 5 got left in.

All the mummies gathered in a circle. They were very excited.

A sound began. A strange, low
vibration which grew louder
HMMMMMMMMM M M M M M M MMM
and louder.
MMMMMMMMMMMMMMM
and louder
MMMMMMMMM!

The Egypt room began to hum and
buzz.

Objects rattled in their glass cases

and the air around the circle
seemed to glow.

Suddenly the Great-Grandaddy
mummy
raised his
hands...

and the
mummyhumming
stopped.

82, Spode Road.
The jewel is there –
a young girl has it.

I think!

The circle broke up.

Well, I'm glad *that's* sorted out.

Me too –
Goodnight.

But....

Good luck
my boy!

But how...?

But all the other mummies were asleep.

Chapter Five

Mo was just nodding off to sleep, when she heard a noise outside her bedroom window.

Mo heaved herself out of bed
and shivered over
to the window.

But it wasn't that Glen Tring
mucking about.

Mo Jones was not a girl who easily lost her nerve. She threw open the window and hissed:

'What do you think you're doing on my bedroom windowsill?'

'I'm a mummy in trouble,' said Tut.

'I know you are,' Mo said. 'You're in trouble with me!'

'You don't understand!' Tut whined. I've lost my . . .'

Mo's dad was not a happy man.
'What's all this noise?' he growled.

Dad flumped back to his room.

Mo turned and gasped,
'What are you *doing*?' she hissed.
'I'm looking for my jewel!'
Tut wailed.

He looked in the drawers,
in the
fishbowl,

under the
bed.

Mo lost her temper.

'Look, I've got an idea,' said Mo,
'You sleep in the shed. Then
tomorrow, I'll help you find your
stupid jewel. *After* the concert!
Is that a deal?'

Tut thought for a long time.
Finally, he said, 'All right!'

Chapter Six

A new day dawned.

Mo woke with circles under her eyes.

But just to be on the safe side . . .

Mo tiptoed past the shed. Then,
just as she reached the end of the
back lane,

It was a moment of major decision.
Only a complete rotter would run
away and leave poor old Tut waving
feebly on the corner.

34

Mo reached the bus with only
seconds to spare.

She had escaped, but not for long.
Just as Mo was walking up to the
school gates, she heard the now
familiar voice.

'Go away!' Mo growled.
'Someone might see you!'

'They wouldn't recognise me
though,' said Tut, winking.

Not in this
nifty disguise.

Mo took a long hard look at Tut's
'disguise'. It looked a lot like Glen
Tring's bike . . .

And his cap . . .

And his violin!

Chapter Seven

Glen Tring was poorly. He'd felt poorly ever since an Egyptian mummy had asked to borrow his bike. Glen had dropped everything and

run

home.

> It seemed a pity to leave all this stuff lying around – so I borrowed it.

Mo was about to tell him he could just *un*-borrow it, when she saw **Mr Glottiss!**

The headteacher was steaming across
the playground towards them.

You girl!
You're <u>late</u>!
You should be...

Then Mr Glottiss saw Tut.
He stared. 'Who is this?'
he asked, gulping.

Mo crossed her fingers.
'It's Glen Tring, sir.'

'Why is he in all those bandages?'
asked the dreaded Head.

'He fell down some stairs, sir,'
said Mo.

Mo thought
quickly.

Mo left Mr Glottiss gaping like a
goldfish, and dragged Tut into
school.

Chapter Eight

Tut spent the rest of the morning
trying to act like Glen Tring.

It was not easy.

Chapter Nine

It was two o'clock. The concert was about to begin. All the parents and guests were there.

Mr Glottiss was there, too, right in the middle of the front row, next to the Mayor. He looked different though. Odd.

I don't believe it. He's SMILING – sort of.

Mr Glottiss stood up and waited for silence. As soon as he spoke, Mo realised why he'd been smiling.

Welcome he said, to the last St Anne's school concert – *ever*.

The whole audience gasped.

GASP!

St Anne's without the concerts would be like the Queen without corgis.

Mr Glottiss carried on.

It has been decided
(by me)
that music practice takes up
too much valuable school time
and money, and so after today
the orchestra will devote
all their time to normal
lessons.

Mr Glottiss looked around at all the
disappointed faces.

'And now,' he smirked, 'the orchestra will play their first piece, called:

Make A Joyful Noise.'

Chapter Ten

The orchestra played their socks off,
just to show Mr Glottiss.

When they finished their first piece
the applause was deafening.

Then came Mo's big moment. With
Glen still at home gibbering, she
had to play on her own. Would she
be any good?

She was OK.

After that the concert was brilliant.
Better than brilliant.

Mo was tuning up for her second
piece when she heard That Voice . . .

The tall bandaged figure blundered
its way along the second row
of the orchestra.

Tut wriggled in next to Mo waving
Glen's violin.

Tut began to scrape away, making a terrible din. He sawed at the strings, grinning at the audience,

but gradually . . .

Tut gave up.

Unravelling as he went, he waded through panic-stricken young musicians, dragging his chair behind him.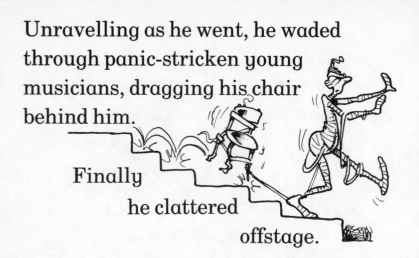

Finally
he clattered
offstage.

The orchestra
was in tears.

The audience
was in fits.

The mayor was in the headteacher's office –
shouting.

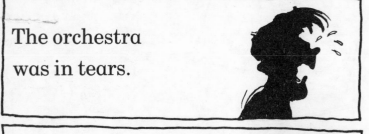

The last
concert
was
over.

Chapter Eleven

Grrrr! That stupid mummy – he's ruined everything.

Mo reached deep into her bag. She took out the special cloth she kept to wipe her violin strings. Something dropped with a clatter under the chair.

'Ooops,' she thought. 'There goes my dinner money.' But when she looked . . .

It can't be!

it IS!

Tut appeared from nowhere.
'What a relief,' he sighed.

'You're telling me,' said Mo.
'Now you can push off back to the
museum and leave me in peace!'

Chapter Twelve

Remember rule 6? The one we said we'd get to later? Well, rule 6 states:

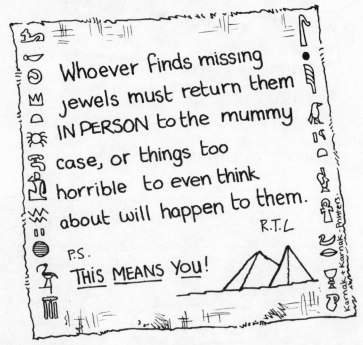

Whoever finds missing jewels must return them IN PERSON to the mummy case, or things too horrible to even think about will happen to them.

R.T.L

P.S.
THIS MEANS YOU!

Karnak + Karnak - Printers.

It's another one from Rameses the Loopy, I'm afraid!

'I'll meet you at your house at seven o'clock,' said Tut. 'And show you how to sneak into the museum.'

Chapter Thirteen

At five past seven Mo heard a sound
like someone walking through
dustbins.

They reached the museum at a
quarter past seven and climbed in
through a window.

CRA·A·ASH!!!

The watchman was out in a flash.

Tut did.

WHANG!

'Let's hurry,' said Mo, 'before he gets that off!'

They raced up to the Egypt room.

What happens now?

I haven't got a clue.

Oh, WHAT !!?

Perhaps we can help?

Chapter Fourteen

The mummies formed a circle around Tut's case and joined hands. As the night watchman bounced around downstairs like a mad pinball, another mummyhumming began. Mo was led to the centre of the circle.

'Now?' said Mo.

'If you don't mind,' the Great-Grandaddy mummy said.

Mo wiggled the jewel

into its proper place.

The Last Bit

The next afternoon,
Mo called in at the museum on her
way home. She went straight to
Tut's case. The label said:

King Tutmahaton

WOW!
You never said
you were a
KING!

You never
asked.

'By the way, I'm sorry I spoiled your concert,' Tut said.

'That's what I came to tell you,' Mo almost jumped up and down with excitement. 'You didn't!'

" The mayor wasn't angry at the orchestra. He <u>loves</u> the concerts. When he was shouting at Mr Glottiss, he was telling him <u>not</u> to stop the concerts or else! And Mr Glottiss is scared stiff of the mayor. "

So you see, Everything is going to be fine.

They chatted on about this and that. Then a museum guide appeared.

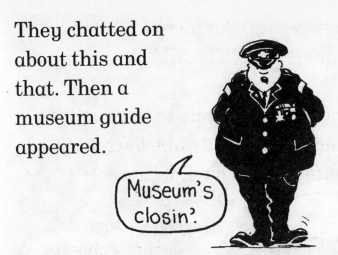

Museum's closin'.

As Mo went out the guide stopped her.

Are you on your own?

Yes.

Who were you just talking to, then?

Just my mummy.

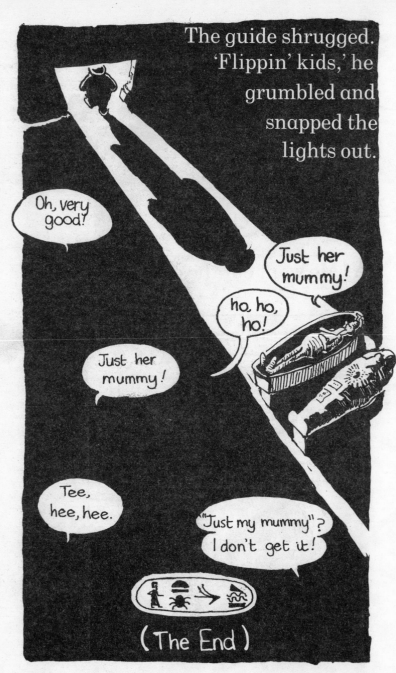